There Was a HOLE

Written by **Adam Lehrhaupt** ○ Illustrated by **Carrie O'Neill**

Lily had a hole.

It ate up all her joy.

Nothing filled it.

Not cookies.

Cake.

Ice cream.

Or even her favorite book.

And the hole kept growing.

Lily got mad.

Daddy noticed.

He tried to help.

He gave her a new toy.

They went to the beach.

They spent a day at Lily's favorite museum.

But nothing fixed the hole.

So Lily stopped trying.

She didn't take part in class.

The hole got bigger.

She ate lunch by herself.

The h**O**le got bigger.

And she sat out while the other kids played her favorite game.

The **hole** got even bigger.

Thomas noticed.

"What's wrong?" he asked.

"I have a h**O**le," Lily said.

"Oh," Thomas whispered.
"Wanna know a secret?

"I have a hole, too."

"What are those?" Lily asked.

"Patches," Thomas said.

"They help you repair the **hole**.

"Want to try?" Thomas asked.

That evening Lily showed the patch to her dad.

They made a new one, together.

And Lily's hole became a bit smaller.

The next day, she showed Thomas.
"It's smaller!" Thomas said.
"You should make more patches."

"I don't want to forget," Lily said.
    "If I patch it completely, will I still remember?"

"You won't forget," Thomas said.
    "But things will get better."

"I'll always remember," Lily thought,
and made a patch so she would.

The next day . . . Lily made another.

Then another.

And another.

Her **hole** began to get smaller.

The patches didn't fix everything.

But they were a start.

There are a lot of reasons someone can feel like they have a hole. Maybe you moved. Perhaps there's a change in your family group such as a sibling going off to school, a separation, or divorce. Maybe you lost a pet, friend, or family member. Unfortunately, whatever the reason for your hole, there's no simple solution to fix it. No magic answer.

Everyone reacts differently to feelings of loss. It's important for you to understand that it's okay to feel the way you do. And it's perfectly fine for your feelings to change, as well. It's just important to remember that the people around you might also be dealing with their own feelings of loss. They might need your assistance as much as you need theirs.

Luckily, there are tools that can help. One of those tools is making patches. Yeah, I know, you don't have an actual hole. But that's okay. It's the process of making patches where the real magic happens.

How to Make a Patch

First, and most important, there's **NO WRONG WAY** to make a patch.
But here are some tips and ideas on how you can make your very own.

1. **Find someone to make your patch with.** Feelings of loss can be compounded by feelings of loneliness. Plus, it's more fun to make patches with someone else. You can even get a group together.

2. **Collect your supplies.** You can make patches out of almost anything. Maybe you want to draw something on paper. Maybe you'd rather sew something. Do you knit? Make stained glass? Weave aluminum foil? Be creative. Think about the person you're making your patch with. What do they like to do? How can you incorporate that into a fun patch?

3. **Be open and honest with your patch buddy.** Making patches is a great time to have a conversation. Ask them how they are feeling. Is something bothering them? Use this time to listen. Are they able to express what they are feeling with words? Does your patch buddy need comfort or reassurance? It's okay if they do. It's also okay if they don't.

4. **Remember to have fun.** Sure, we're talking about how to recover from loss, but that doesn't mean you can never enjoy yourself again. In fact, until you give yourself permission to have fun, it will be very hard for you to mend your hole.

5. **Find a good place to store or display your patch.** I made a big black hole on a piece of paper and I put all my patches on it. Wanna know a secret? It's almost completely covered! You don't need to do the same thing, but you should keep your patches. They're a good way to remember the person, pet, or thing you lost and to remember the person or people who helped you move on.